Contents

KV-191-955

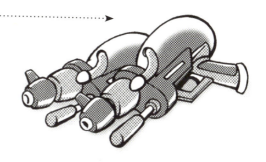

SECRET MISSIONS

Characters

Earthlings

Scott

Thirteen-year-old Scott's favourite things are science and skateboarding – and avoiding his snoopy big sister.

AJ

Scott's daredevil friend AJ is always taking crazy risks, and he has lots of cuts and bruises to show for it.

Rudy

The conscience of the group. He likes woodwork, hanging with Scott and AJ, and his Red Sox cap.

Penny

Scott's fourteen-year-old sister Penny likes to poke her nose into his life – and get him into trouble.

Halycrusians

Inhabitants of the environmentally ravaged planet Halycrus. They live underground, hiding from the vicious mountain swine.

Z-kee

R-cher

T-kwinia

Out of this World

SECRET
MISSIONS

by Keira Wong

illustrated by Douglas Fong

H   A      U   S

This 2009 edition published in the United Kingdom by
Scholastic Ltd
Villiers House
Clarendon Avenue
Leamington Spa
Warwickshire
CV32 5PR

First published in 2007
by Macmillan Education Australia Pty Ltd.

Text by Keira Wong
Illustrations by Douglas Fong
Cover Design Allison Parry
Designed by Matt Lin/Goblin Design
Managing Editor Nicola Robinson

Out of this World: Secret Missions
ISBN 978 1407 10105 7

Printed by Tien Wah Press, Singapore

1 2 3 4 5 6 7 8 9   9 0 1 2 3 4 5 6 7 8

H A L Y C R U S

chapter 1

An Argument

I could smell it. I didn't even have to see it to know that it was behind me.

Watch out! Z-kee's voice entered my mind just before a mountain swine lunged at me. I ducked under its claws. Phew, that was close!

Through the darkness, I spied Z-kee's yellow skin. So did the mountain swine. But it couldn't see me. We both started towards Z-kee but I skidded in front of it and stuck out my foot. It nearly fell on top of me. I somersaulted out of the way just in time. There was no way I was going to get stuck under that stinky thing!

The swine skidded into the rock where Z-kee was collecting bejais, little jewels found in large rocks. I grabbed Z-kee's long yellow arm. His cold, clammy suction fingers held my hand tightly as we tumbled down one of the entrance tunnels, towards Z-kee's underground cave den.

Whoa, I was having too many close calls. I had barely escaped my one-on-one battle with the mountain swine just a few hours before. Finding

out that soft drink burned their ugly blue hairy bodies had been a great discovery.

It was a great discovery but you are putting us at risk, intruder. A dark purple belly glowed in front of me, as I lay flat on my back on the stone floor. R-cher. His glowing belly told me it was his thought echoing inside my head. His words told me that once again he had read my mind. I was learning to project my thoughts – but hide them? I couldn't do that yet.

R-cher stared at me with his narrow, dark eyes, his limbs stretched out in front of him. He loved calling me "intruder" in front of the other Halycrusians. I had a few names for him, too.

R-cher, calm down. Z-kee's belly turned a pale purple as his thought entered my mind.

The two of them looked so different. Z-kee's long yellow arms flopped by his side and rested

on his pot belly. His eyes were dark like R-cher's, but wide. Their bellies changed from purple to yellow as they spoke to each other, but no thoughts entered my mind. They were blocking them from me.

I pinched myself. It was hard to believe that this was not a dream. I was actually in another world, a planet with a dying sun. I had battled the mountain swine, the vicious creatures that forced the Halycrusians to live underground. The Halycrusians' only food was bejais, which also gave off light when joined together. The most powerful, brightest and best-tasting bejais were above the city, where the dangerous mountain swine now lived. The swine were always ready to gore anything with their sharp, white horns.

Even though it was really dangerous, I'd had an awesome time trying to collect bejais and battling the swine! It was unreal. And I couldn't believe that I'd actually made the portal that connected Earth to Halycrus. (OK, so I didn't really "make" it. I fell over in the scrapyard and the fake snot I made for my science project mysteriously created the portal when it smashed

on the ground. But if I wasn't clumsy, it would never have happened!)

Scott was just helping me use the tools he brought. Z-kee's voice entered my mind again.

Halycrusians had incredible powers. Not only could they communicate by mind-reading, but they could mould rocks with their bare hands, as if it were play-dough. That's how they got the bejais out of the rocks – they just pulled it out.

I had brought hammers and chisels from Earth, so that we could chip pieces off the rocks quickly, and buckets to carry them down to the caves. I'd thought the Halycrusians could pull the bejais from the chipped-off rocks back underground, safe from the swine. But so far it hadn't worked out that way.

Z-kee, I know others are not happy with the intruder putting us at risk. R-cher pointed to the far side of the cave city. I saw his group of friends. Of course they would agree with anything R-cher said! Again, I was blocked from Z-kee and R-cher's conversation. I thought it was time for me to go home.

Yes, you should have gone home ages ago. R-cher's belly turned a dark purple when his thought entered my mind.

I stared down at him. He was half my size. I was not afraid of him.

Scott and I have been making plans. It won't be so dangerous next time we face the swine. Z-kee's belly changed to a pale purple. He turned to me. *I will see you soon, like we planned.*

Making secret plans, Z-kee? We are not happy with this. R-cher sounded angry. It was definitely time for me to leave.

I grabbed a small foil packet out of my backpack and opened it up. My fake snot/portal mixture sparkled back at me. This was the last of it. I'd have to make some more. I threw the packet at the stone wall to create the portal back to Earth. It pulsated and glimmered green.

See ya, Z-kee! I hoisted the backpack on to my shoulders and touched the glowing green wall. A hot throbbing rushed through me as my hand, arm and body disappeared into the portal.

chapter 2

The Wrong Portal

SPLAT!

The cold air of the scrapyard greeted me as I landed on Earth. It was a nice change. Halycrus was so hot and the air was hard to breathe. I knelt down, breathing in the chilly air. It felt strange to come back home. Pins and needles tingled all over my body and my head really hurt.

It was dark. Would Mum be furious with me? I looked at my watch – six o'clock. It was dinner time. The kitchen would be filled with my six brothers and sisters. Nobody would notice if I sneaked back in. I hoped.

I picked up my skateboard, which I had left behind a tree, and skated home as fast as I could.

Quickly but quietly, I climbed up the trellis underneath my bedroom window.

"Where were you?"

Caught! I still had one foot out the window. My older sister Penny stood in my bedroom doorway, her hands on her hips. She narrowed her eyes.

"You've been gone since breakfast," she said.

"Since when have you been so interested in what I do?" I tossed my board and backpack in

my wardrobe. I didn't want her to ask any more questions.

Penny stuck her tongue out at me. "You've been acting so strange lately. You'd better not be lying to Mum and Dad about where you've been. You're going to get in trouble otherwise. What are you up to?"

I dodged past her and walked down the stairs towards the dining room. Her questions were making me nervous. Mum and Dad would never believe me if I told them where I'd really been.

"Hi, Scotty." Dad smiled and put a plate of spaghetti in front of me. No one asked me where I had been. In fact, no one asked me anything except to pass the pepper. When Mum gave me dessert after dinner, I took a big spoonful and poked my tongue out at Penny. Man, did it taste good!

"Yes! We can really come this time?" AJ's eyes and smile were so wide I thought his face would crack. Rudy, my other best friend, didn't look as excited. I knew AJ wanted to come to share in my adventures. Rudy was coming to keep an eye on AJ.

"Yep, Z-kee said it was OK! R-cher is not crash hot on the idea, so don't expect a hug and a kiss when we get there."

It was the middle of the night and we were in my garage. I had to keep telling AJ to keep his voice down in case my parents – or worse, Penny – woke up. I'd decided to go to Halycrus while everyone was in bed so nobody would notice we were missing for hours on end. We would leave Halycrus again in time to get back home before anyone woke up.

"I've brought all the soft drink cans." Thirty cans of soft drink were piled in the wooden trolley that Rudy had made in woodwork class. "I don't know if Mum believed me when I said they were for your 'science project'."

"What's in the garbage bags?" AJ pulled out a long-sleeved black T-shirt.

"That's one of Dad's botched deliveries from a few days ago," I said, putting the bag in Rudy's trolley.

Dad owned a courier service. Usually his botched deliveries piled up in the garage, worthless to anyone until we threw them out. But now they were essential to my plans for helping the Halycrusians battle the mountain swine.

"Perfect timing, really," I said. "You see, the mountain swine spot the Halycrusians easily because of their yellow skin. But they can't see me because of my black hair and eyes. The T-shirts are to disguise them. That's why I told you guys to wear dark clothes."

"Let's go now! I can't wait to see this place!" AJ skated around the garage. "Where's your portal mixture?"

I pulled a handful of foil packets from my backpack. Last time, the mountain swine almost took off with my only portal packet and nearly left me stranded on Halycrus. I wasn't taking any chances, so I'd made about fifteen batches. AJ opened one up.

"It looks so real. Or did you just sneeze in it?"

Rudy poked AJ. "It looks different from before. Isn't it meant to be green?"

I nodded and put the packets back in the backpack. "It was only coloured green to make it look like flu snot. I used Penny's make-up. She almost killed me when she found out! I didn't take any this time. I don't want her asking any more questions than she is already. But it's all the same stuff, in all the same amounts. That's all we need."

It didn't take us very long to get to the scrapyard. AJ sprinted the whole way.

"We're here! Let's go!" Icy air blew out of AJ's mouth. "Can I make the portal?"

I handed him a portal packet.

"Just open it up and smash it on that rock over there."

AJ smashed the packet on the rock and fell silent as the rock began to throb. He was impressed, but to me the rock looked all wrong. It usually shimmered green, but that must have been because the fake snot was a green colour. Now the rock was bright white, almost blinding me. The glow had never been this intense. This wasn't right...

"AJ, don't!" But it was too late. AJ's hand had already disappeared into the rock. Suddenly, his body was sucked in and he was gone!

"What's wrong, Scott?" Rudy asked. "Why did you tell him not to touch it?"

I grabbed hold of Rudy and touched the rock. Burning pain shot down my arm. I wanted to pull away but I knew I had to get to AJ. The pain became worse as Rudy and I were pulled into who knows where.

chapter 3

Mudland

Rudy and I landed face first in mud.

"I dink I broke my nove!"

The trolley and garbage bag landed on top of AJ with a thud. He was holding a muddy hand to his face.

"Are you OK, AJ?" I grabbed a T-shirt from the bag and gave it to him to wipe his face.

AJ wiped the mud from his eyes. "Is this Halycrus? I thought you said it was warm. It's more freezing than the scrapyard!"

Dark vines and small brown nuts hung from tall trees. The ground was muddy. The air was cold. And the sun was shining.

This was not Halycrus.

Suddenly, something swooped down on us. We all ducked, our arms covering our heads. Loud screeches filled the air. My ears ached. Ow! It was worse than fingernails on a blackboard. WHOOSH! Something grabbed at my hair. It pulled harder and I was lifted off the ground!

"Scott!" Rudy shouted.

He grabbed my leg and pulled me down. My hair was almost torn from my head. I took my backpack off my shoulders and tried to hit the creature with it. AJ threw a soft drink can and it smacked the creature in the face. It let me go. The three of us ran and hid behind a tree. My head was stinging.

"What is it?" AJ whispered, pointing to the horrible creature that had grabbed me.

I didn't know. It was furry, with two round heads and wings. A claw stuck out from its abdomen. One of the heads let out a loud screech and the creature circled towards

our supplies, which were still lying in the mud. It grabbed my backpack with its claw and flew off towards a gigantic tree in the distance.

"Where are we, Scott?" Rudy looked scared and his face was pale. I could see every one of his freckles.

"Those two-headed things were scary ... but cool." AJ's eyes were wide with disbelief. He looked frightened, but I think he was enjoying it.

"I don't know. Something was wrong with that portal mixture," I said. "It didn't look right. Oh no! That creature's got the backpack!"

"So? Better your backpack than your head!" AJ said.

"It's not that!" I looked desperately towards the tree. "The portal mixture was in there!"

"Again, so what?" AJ shook my shoulder. "The mixture was wrong, remember? It's a good thing they took it."

"But how are we supposed to get back home, AJ?" Rudy yelled. "We got here by that mixture and that's what's going to get us home!"

We looked glumly towards the gigantic tree. Smoke was coming from the top of it. The winged two-heads circled the tree, as if it were prey. Their screeches echoed through the jungle. In between the screeches we heard loud thumps, like someone banging a drum. I rubbed my head. A few hairs came loose in my fingertips.

"What if those things come back?" I asked. I felt awful. I had dragged us into this place because I couldn't get the portal mixture right! I had put my best friends in danger. What an idiot.

"It's OK, Scotty," Rudy said. He patted me on the back.

AJ squeezed my shoulder reassuringly. "We just have to watch out for them. But I wish my mouth wasn't full of mud!"

"Lucky we brought the drink," I said gloomily.

We washed our mouths out with some of the soft drink.

"Well, I came here for an adventure and I'm going to get one!" AJ grinned. "We're getting that mixture back. We're going to that tree."

"It's looks so far away," Rudy said.

"Well, what else are we going to do? Wait for someone to pick us up and take us home?" AJ squinted towards the gigantic tree. "It's not that far. Come on, guys!"

AJ threw the garbage bag over his back. He packed up the trolley and tried to drag it through the mud. That was never going to work. I rushed to help him carry it. The mud was thick. We could hardly walk through it! Rudy grabbed the bag from AJ, while AJ and I carried the trolley full of soft drink cans.

We stuck close to the trees in case the winged two-heads came back. The drums kept on beating, but we didn't have the time to think about that, because the mud was like quicksand. Rudy got stuck up to his waist in a pothole. It took all our strength to pull him out.

AJ found an easier way to get through the mud – sliding! "YEE-HAH!" he yelled.

That gave me an idea. "Hey, watch this!" I clambered up a tree and grabbed one of the thick vines hanging from its branches. I swung myself down to the ground and then let go, grabbing Rudy's ankle on the way. Rudy fell on his back and I pulled him with me, sliding across the mud.

"You just gave me the biggest wedgie!" Rudy laughed.

"Catch this, Scott!"

AJ swung from a vine and threw a mud ball in my face. Then he let go and slid away. He was gone before I had a chance to throw a mud ball back. I grabbed a vine. Rudy pulled me back and pushed me hard to slide me into AJ. The force of our collision sent AJ gliding twice as fast as before.

We were so busy playing mud dominoes that we didn't notice a shadow circling above us. It wasn't until we heard an ear-piercing screech that we looked up and saw a winged two-head grab AJ by the shirt. Then it took him away.

chapter 4

An Exchange

"**N**ow what?" Rudy was pale even under all the mud caked on his face. "Those things will have eaten AJ by the time we get to him!"

I didn't answer him. If only I had made the mixture correctly, we'd be on Halycrus, instead of dealing with these flying two-heads. Sure, battling mountain swine wasn't a walk in the park, but at least I knew how to handle them!

Rudy and I trudged through the mud, scared and worried. Sliding would have been easier and faster, but it just didn't feel right to do it.

I looked up and saw the two-heads flying over a treeless patch to our right. I grabbed a vine and slid in their direction.

"What are you doing?" Rudy yelled before he slid after me.

We came to a halt in the treeless patch. The two-heads screeched.

"Are you crazy?" Rudy said. "They're going to grab us!"

"Good! They'll take us where they took AJ!"

Crouching down, I threw a mud ball at the two-heads. I covered my head when they swooped towards me. They weren't grabbing me by the hair this time!

A claw grabbed me by the shirt collar, lifting me high above the ground.

Another grabbed Rudy by his ankle, hanging him upside down.

The third grabbed Rudy's trolley.

The two-heads flapped their great wings and headed towards the giant tree. The drumming

got louder and I heard weird chanting. When we got closer, I saw a fire next to a wooden platform in the middle of the tree. Then I saw AJ standing on a pile of leaves. He was all right! But then he got smaller. My winged two-head was taking me away from him! I looked towards Rudy. His two-head was taking him in the wrong direction as well!

No! Left, towards AJ! I thought, pointing towards AJ. Could mind-reading work on this planet too? Suddenly my flying two-head turned a head towards me. He understood my pleas!

Can we go down there, to that boy on the pile of leaves? I thought.

The winged two-head screeched, and its echo "spoke" to me through the bass of the drumming. *Down there? And your other friend?* It bobbed its head towards Rudy.

Yes!

It screeched loudly towards Rudy's winged two-head. *Follow me, quick! Before the ceremony!* Its screech echoed through the chanting as it swooped towards AJ.

I was dropped next to AJ, on the pile of leaves. Rudy landed head first. His trolley crashed beside him, scattering cans everywhere.

"Hey!" AJ grinned. "You guys came to rescue me! This place rocks! Those flying two-heads aren't so bad. But check out those guys!" He pointed towards the fire.

Big, hairy balls stood in a semicircle around the platform, stomping the ground and chanting. If coconuts were alive, this is what they would

look like, with little white arms and legs. Could this place get any more weird?

The flying creatures screeched in time with the chanting. *Hail! Hail!* Their screeches echoed through the drumming.

I looked closer at the platform. The coconut men were bowing to my backpack!

"They think it's a god!" Rudy laughed. "What a joke!"

"They almost squashed me when I tried to get the portal mixtures from the backpack," AJ said. "But it's not the mixtures they want. It's the backpack! They gave me back the

mixtures and traded me these in exchange for the backpack to, um, worship."

AJ held out his hand. Five small brown nuts lay in his palm.

"What are they? Food?" I asked.

"I dunno," AJ said. "Nice souvenir though! Hey, look. The coconut people have some too. Big ones."

Three coconut men were carrying a huge brown nut each. Their little arms could barely wrap around them. They hurled the nuts towards the fire.

BOOM!

The nuts exploded and a huge cloud of smoke floated from the fire. Big flames flared, licking at the edges of the platform.

"Excellent!" AJ's eyes lit up with mischief. "These are little fire starters!" He threw one on the ground.

BANG!

It exploded right near a coconut man's leg. He jumped back from the flare but continued to chant and bow.

"Think it's time to go home?" I asked. "They don't seem to care if we're here or not, now that they've got their god."

AJ pocketed the rest of the nuts and we started to move off. I waved to the coconut men. They ignored me.

"Do we need to smash the mixture on a rock? Will it take us back to the scrapyard or to where we landed in Mudland?" Rudy asked.

"I don't know," I said. "On Halycrus, I smashed it on the cave city floor the first time I wanted to go back home, then in Z-kee's cave den the next time. I arrived in the scrapyard both times. I think it just needs to be smashed against something hard so it explodes and gets us back to the yard."

"We've got so many dud mixtures that it's worth a try." AJ smashed the mixture against the tree trunk. It shimmered white.

We were going home.

I climbed up to my bedroom, leaving muddy footprints on the trellis. It was five in the morning. I tiptoed past Penny's bedroom. Her door was open, which was strange. Penny was always thinking someone was going to read her diary and kept her room locked whether she was in or out of it. Penny's blond hair poked out of the blankets but she was asleep – I think.

My body felt like it was sunburnt, stinging with pain. I couldn't believe I got the portal mixture wrong. I wasn't going to make that mistake again. Although, secretly, I knew I'd like to go back to Mudland.

chapter 5

The Make-up Mission

I decided to go back to Halycrus the next night.

"Are you crazy?" Rudy said when I told him my plan. "What happens if we end up in a worse place than Mudland?"

"We just went through the wrong portal, that's all."

"You said it was the same stuff as the Halycrus portal."

"It wasn't. I didn't do it right. I know what was missing. The first mixture was green and the portal to Halycrus was green. *This* mixture was white and the portal to Mudland was white. I didn't use Penny's make-up. That's the missing ingredient to the Halycrus portal!"

"How are you going to get Penny's make-up?" Rudy asked. "Wouldn't she wonder why her *brother* wants to use her *make-up*?"

"Well, how else are we going to get the make-up? Buy some?" I laughed.

AJ's eyes lit up.

"I'm *not* going to buy make-up," I said. "I'd rather ask Penny straight out if I could borrow some of hers."

Both Rudy and AJ raised their eyebrows. They were close to my family. Penny was like a sister to them and they knew her as well as I did.

"OK," I grumbled. "How much do you think eyeshadow costs?"

✪ ✪ ✪

Mum was reading my baby sister, Bella, a story. She looked up as the three of us approached.

"Hi, boys. You look worried."

"Um, Mum." I rubbed the toe of my trainer into the carpet, not looking at her. "I was wondering what sort of eyeshadow Penny wears."

I heard a snigger from the doorway. I turned around. Dean,

one of my younger brothers, smirked at us.

"Make-up? You guys are so weird." Dean pulled his ugliest face, then ran out of the room before I had time to explain myself.

"It's not for me!" I called after him, too late. He'd keep on teasing me for weeks. Oh well.

"Why do you want to know, honey?" asked Mum.

Bella crawled to Rudy. He picked her up and she grabbed at his hat.

Shucks, I didn't want to lie to Mum.

"Is it for a present? Aren't you sweet?" Her smile became brighter and wider.

This was making it very hard.

"It's actually for our science project, Mrs W," AJ volunteered. "Remember the doll – I mean mannequin – Scotty was working on? Eyeshadow is one of the main snot ingredients but we don't want to use Penny's."

I grinned at AJ. Your best friends always know when to save you.

"Of course! It's called Lime Ice. You get it from the pharmacy down the road. Just take some money out of my purse. I'll buy it for you."

"Thanks, Mum!"

I breathed a sigh of relief as the three of us skated down the road towards the pharmacy. But I got nervous again as we entered the shop. Rudy shrugged and looked awkwardly at some lipsticks by the counter. AJ pretended to be really interested in looking over Rudy's shoulder.

"Are you boys OK?" A young shop assistant smiled at us. "I'm Molly. How can I help?"

I swallowed nervously. Rudy nudged me and nodded.

"Um, do you have any Lime Ice eyeshadow?" I whispered.

"What was that?" the assistant said loudly, looking bored. "You have to speak up."

Out of the corner of my eye, I saw some older girls from my school.

"Lime Ice," I said in my lowest voice, hoping it was loud enough for the assistant to hear. "Eyeshadow."

One of the girls waved to Rudy. She was in his woodwork class.

"Lime Ice eyeshadow?" the shop assistant asked. Suddenly I had her full attention. "What for?"

I was ready to run out of the shop and ask Penny for her make-up. The girls were looking curiously at us now. I heard a giggle.

"Hey, Larissa!" Rudy said loudly, trying to speak over the assistant's voice. He walked over to the girls. "Did you end up asking Mr Holden if you can use the workshop after school?" Then he led them out of the shop.

Friends. You've got to love them!

I handed over Mum's money, shocked at the price. It would have cost us a whole week's allowance! (No wonder Penny was angry when she saw me spilling it all over the floor.)

We hurried outside. Rudy was still talking to the girls. AJ hid the package behind his back before they asked what we'd bought.

Rudy gave us a knowing look and jumped on his skateboard. "See you at school! Bye!" he called over his shoulder.

We skated away as fast as we could. AJ kick-flipped his board over the kerb, a perfect trick. Always the showman…

"All right, here we go again!" AJ punched the air with his fist.

Rudy set his trolley down next to a tree in the scrapyard. The cans of soft drink were still covered in mud. So were AJ's trousers. He obviously hadn't changed his clothes. ("Why dirty another pair in case we end up somewhere worse?" he said. That didn't do much for my self-esteem.)

"I brought some water pistols so we can just spray the mountain swine with the soft drink," Rudy said.

"That's a really good idea!" I said.

"We make a great team!" AJ said. "Rudy, you were ace handling Larissa and her friends! And now we have the vital ingredient for the portal. Hey, maybe we should put something else in the portal mixture and see where it takes us!"

"No, no more," Rudy said. "I want to know what Halycrus is like first."

I threw down the portal packet and the rock shimmered a familiar green.

"This is it, guys," I said, grabbing my new backpack, which was full of T-shirts. "See you soon."

AJ and Rudy's faces started to fade and the tingling sensation took over my body. It felt like my body had been separated into millions of pieces and was slowly being put back together. My feet found solid ground. I saw Halycrus's dark sky and felt its warm air.

AJ landed next to me. "Man, it's hot!" he said, taking his jumper off. His T-shirt was bright red.

PLOP! Rudy arrived, his trolley toppled over and the soft drinks tumbled out. AJ chased a can that rolled behind a bejais rock.

"AJ, put your jumper back on. Your T-shirt's too bright. The mountain swine will spot you straight away!" I yelled after him.

Too late!

The ground vibrated and a mountain swine bellowed.

"AJ, get out of the way!" I yelled.

It charged right at him. He dodged out of its way and ran up the hill, the mountain swine hot on his heels. Then they both disappeared from sight.

chapter 6

Rescue!

Rudy and I started filling up water pistols with soft drink. We both knew what we had to do. Our tried and true teamwork had to get us out of another sticky situation.

We sprinted up the hill, looking over our shoulders for mountain swine.

"There's AJ!" Rudy yelled.

AJ was facing a swine. Another swine was scraping the ground behind him, ready to charge.

"AJ, behind you!" Rudy yelled.

AJ didn't actually look like he needed our help. "Hi-yahh!" He high-kicked the mountain swine on its pig snout. "I knew you guys would come to rescue me again!" He grinned at us before he back-flipped and punched the other swine in the face. I wished I had learned karate with AJ when he'd asked me to.

"Just spray the swine with the soft drink!" I shouted to Rudy. "It burns their hair off, remember?"

Rudy quickly climbed the bejais rock behind the first swine and soaked it with soft drink. The swine bellowed. There was a loud sizzle and huge chunks of blue hair dropped off its back. It bellowed again and ran away.

We'd done it!

"All right, Rudy!" I yelled, punching the air. I looked in AJ's direction. There was still one more swine to deal with.

"This is for your smelly breath!" AJ kicked the second mountain swine in the snout. The swine scraped the ground and lowered its head.

"It's going to charge!" I sprinted towards him.

AJ grabbed the mountain swine's sharp horns and flipped himself on to its back! "Chuck me your pistol, Scott!" he yelled.

I couldn't believe he did that! I decided on the spot to sign up for karate classes when we got

back home! I threw my pistol and AJ caught it with his left hand. He sprayed soft drink all over the swine's back and down its face. It bellowed and reared back, but AJ kept his balance perfectly. I could tell he was enjoying himself.

"And this is for your ugly face!" AJ gave a final squirt before jumping off the swine's back. It reared on its hind legs before running away.

"Yeah!" Rudy jumped down from the rock and high-fived us. "That was awesome!"

And then I smelled them. The stench was so bad, I knew there was more than one.

"Um, guys," I said.

I slowly turned around. Rudy and AJ stopped slapping each other on the back and their shouts quietened.

"Oh … my…" Rudy's jaw dropped open.

Ten mountain swine stared back at us. And man, did they look ticked off! Their eyes glowed redder than ever and their yellow claws looked sharper. The leader had a black mark on its face where AJ had burned its hair off with soft drink.

"Rudy, do you have any more soft drink in your pistol?" AJ whispered. "Because I used all mine on that angry-looking one."

"Not enough for all of them," Rudy said, turning pale.

The leader swine scraped the ground and bellowed.

"Run!" I yelled. The three of us raced down the hill. The swine galloped after us.

I knew there was an entrance tunnel to the cave city somewhere. I blindly turned right. I didn't know where I was.

There wasn't enough time to look for a tunnel. The bellowing swine were right on our tail. Wait ... the swine had terrible eyesight. They couldn't

see me because of my dark colouring. Rudy's cap covered his light hair. So how could they see us now?

A flash of red caught my eye. AJ was right behind me, his red T-shirt leading the swine towards us!

"AJ!" I shouted, pointing at his shirt.

"Oh, sorry, I forgot! My T-shirt!" He whipped off his shirt, balled it up and threw it as far as he could. The mountain swine swerved in the direction of the red streak.

We raced to where we had left our supplies.

"Where's our stuff?" Rudy gasped, inhaling on his asthma puffer. "It's gone! Our stuff has gone!"

He was right.

The trolley was empty.

Our soft drinks were gone.

Even the T-shirts were missing.

"Uh-oh," AJ said. "They're coming back. It's pretty hard to throw a T-shirt far! Just run!"

I ran to my left. Rudy ran to the right. AJ hesitated for a second, not knowing which one of us to follow. It was a second too late. The group of mountain swine surrounded him. He had no choice now. For the first time ever, AJ looked scared. He stood still, never taking his eyes off the swine. He reached into his pocket and a devilish smile crept over his face. Quick as a flash, AJ pulled something from his pocket.

BANG!

It sounded like a firecracker. He'd thrown the Mudland nuts! So it was a good thing I stuffed up the portal mixture!

A small spark flew up and a puff of smoke circled AJ. The swine were stunned. AJ crawled between their legs.

But the swine were stunned for only a second. The leader swine stomped its paw to the ground. Its claw snagged AJ's muddy pants and yanked him backwards.

Suddenly, a flash of bright yellow appeared in front of us. It was T-kwinia.

Now it's my turn to save you! she "said" in my mind. I'd once saved her from the swine, when we were gathering bejais together.

Her bright yellow skin caught the swine's attention and they raced towards her. She galloped up the hill, her long arms pulling her short body forward. She looked like a yellow bullet hurtling through the air!

"They're gaining on her!" Rudy said, taking another puff on his inhaler.

The leader swine swiped at T-kwinia but she disappeared down an entry tunnel. It skidded into a bejais rock behind the tunnel. The other swine collided with it.

I heard a loud sizzle and all ten of the swine bellowed. Huge chunks of blue hair had fallen to the ground. What was going on? I couldn't see anything. What was burning them? I squinted in the darkness. It was the Halycrusians! They were wearing the black T-shirts and spraying the swine with water pistols!

The swine gave one final bellow, rocking the ground. Then they ran away for the last time.

They have gone! Z-kee's voice suddenly entered my mind. *Victory!*

chapter 7

Back to Earth

"**A**re you guys all right?" I asked aloud.

Rudy and AJ were pale. They looked dizzy. Rudy kept puffing on his inhaler.

"I hear voices, Scotty," AJ whispered to me. "But not in my ears, in my head!"

"It's OK. I told you, this is how they speak to each other."

"We know," Rudy said. "It's just weird. And it's so dry and hot. It's hard to breathe."

Your friends must have a bejais. Z-kee pointed to a pile on the ground.

The pile of marble-sized balls sparkled with every colour of the rainbow. I looked up. Multicoloured disco balls (lots of bejais joined together) shone brightly. The Halycrusians had been busy collecting from above ground while I was away.

I plucked a blue and green bejais from the pile. (I avoided the orange ones. They tasted horrible.) I gave one each to AJ and Rudy. They popped them in their mouths and their eyes widened. I knew the bejais were growing.

Rudy coughed and AJ laughed. The bejais had exploded in their mouths, leaving a tingling feeling.

"That was weird!" AJ said. "Can I have another one? I feel a lot better now."

We have plenty now, thanks to Scott! Z-kee said, patting AJ's shoulder with his long yellow arm. He could barely reach; AJ was the tallest of us. *You were great with the swine!*

AJ smiled and said nothing.

Scott and I had talked about the black shirts. That's how we knew to take them. Z-kee's thought echoed in my head.

A few seconds later, his voice entered my mind again. *That was T-kwinia.*

What was going on? Who was Z-kee talking to now?

AJ. Z-kee turned to me. *He has learned very quickly to channel his thoughts only to me.*

AJ laughed and his voice entered my head.

I told you to go to karate, Scott. They teach you mind control and focus.

"What's going on?" Rudy asked aloud.

I'm glad I wasn't the only one who didn't get the mind-reading thing.

We spent a while eating and practising our thought channelling. Most of the Halycrusians were fascinated by AJ and Rudy, but I noticed R-cher and his gang didn't come near us. They sat close by but avoided our eyes. That was fine with me.

I think we have to get home, I said. *It's early in the morning on Earth now.*

I hope Scott brings you back. Z-kee patted us all on our shoulders. *AJ, you need to teach us your moves to fight the swine. And that wooden trolley was very good. It would make bringing the bejais down to our city much easier.*

I made that. I can make heaps more for you. Rudy's voice entered my mind. He wasn't speaking out loud this time. *It won't take me very long.*

You made the trolley? R-cher's low voice entered my mind. This was the first time he had said anything to us. His belly turned a deep purple.

Yeah, it's easy. Rudy shrugged.

R-cher shot me a dirty look.

The intrud – um, Scott made us use buckets last time, but they were too heavy to carry when we filled them with bejais rocks. We take them down the tunnel one at a time now. That trolley was very easy to push. Could you make some more?

Weird. R-cher didn't call me "intruder". He sounded, well, nice. I didn't care. I still didn't trust him.

Why not, Scott? R-cher patted me on the shoulder. *We battled the mountain swine together last time, remember?*

I thought it was your fault he had to battle the swine – and by himself, I might add. AJ towered over R-cher.

R-cher's eyes narrowed for just a second. Then he looked at AJ with a blank face.

Oh … yes. Scott was great. He is a big help to Halycrus. So are you and Trudy.

Rudy. AJ shot him a dirty look. Then his face went blank. *Well, I had an awesome time! But we have to get back home. We'll see you next time! Thanks for saving us, T-kwinia!*

It was my pleasure! One good turn deserves another. T-kwinia's belly turned pale purple as she said her goodbyes.

R-cher was standing really close to me. I felt like telling him to push off, but it didn't matter. We were going home after another victory!

I pulled the portal packet out of my backpack and opened it up. *See you, guys! We"ll be back soon!*

I smashed the packet on the stone wall and it began to glow green. Rudy touched the wall

and slowly disappeared. AJ followed him. When it was my turn, I thought I felt something cold grab my ankle. But the hot throbbing took over my body as I went down the portal towards home.

AJ and Rudy were waiting for me back at the scrapyard. AJ was jumping up and down in excitement. "That was so cool! Man, it's nice and cool here. It was so hot there! I still have a headache. My body feels all tingly but not like bejais tingly. That was a weird thing, hey?"

We grabbed our skateboards from behind the tree and skated home. It was five in the morning. Something yellow flashed between the trees, but I quickly forgot about it as we talked about our journey to Halycrus.

We discussed our plans for battling the mountain swine, and what to take to Halycrus the next time we went. Our teamwork had helped us survive the swine and the Mudland disaster – and we'd even bought make-up together! Helping the Halycrusians was great. But helping them with my friends was even better!

Secret Missions Portalopedia

Bejais The Halycrusians' only food. It is found in rocks.

Coconut men Inhabitants of Mudland. Their correct name is unknown but Scott and his friends know them as "coconut men" because of their shape.

Halycrus An alternative world.

Halycrusians Inhabitants of Halycrus.

Mind-reading The ability to read another person's thoughts. This is a very handy skill if you cannot understand someone's language, because the thoughts do not need language.

Mountain swine A massive blue hairy creature from Halycrus. Dangerous.

Mudland An alternative world.

Portal An opening into an alternative world.

Portal mixture A mixture of materials which opens portals into alternative worlds.

Winged two-head Large two-headed flying animal with a single clawed foot. Inhabitant of Mudland.